Lulu's House, Wagtail Town, The World, The Universe

Me →

Alfie ← My very best friend

Pom →
She always looks on the bright side

Harvey →
He is good at tricks

Yumi →
She thinks she is a fairytale princess

Otto →
He collects beetles

Dear Reader,
Have you ever been to Wagtail Town? It is the best place EVER! You will meet my very best friend, Alfie, and all my other friends: Yumi, Pom, Bonnie, Harvey, and Otto.
We all go to Miss Ellie's New Tricks School and every day is fun, fun, fun! Come and see!
Lots of love from
Lulu

Bonnie
She's Miss Messy

the Little Dog with BIG ideas!

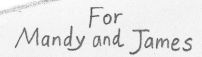

For
Mandy and James

First published in hardback in Great Britain by
HarperCollins Children's Books in 2012
First published in paperback in 2012

1 3 5 7 9 10 8 6 4 2

ISBN: 978-0-00-742515-0

HarperCollins Children's Books is a division of HarperCollins Publishers Ltd.

Text and illustrations copyright © Emma Chichester Clark 2012

Visit our website at: www.harpercollins.co.uk

Printed in China

Lulu's house

Pom's house

Harvey's house

Wagtail Town

Lulu and the Best Cake Ever!

Emma Chichester Clark

HarperCollins Children's Books

Over the hills and far away there's a lovely place called Wagtail Town where Lulu lives. One day Lulu was having a good idea!

"Oooh la la!" she cried.

"I mus

ell Alfie!"

Alfie is Lulu's very best friend.

"Alfie!" said Lulu. "I've got the **best** idea **ever!**"

"Another one?" asked Alfie, because even though Lulu is only a little dog, she has a lot of big ideas.

"Yes!" cried Lulu. "You're going to help me make the **best** cake in the whole town and **win** the school cake competition! Hurry up and come over!"

When Alfie arrived, Lulu hopped on to the back of his scooter.

"We're going to win!
  We're going to win!
    We're going to win!"
she sang as they set off to the shops.

"Lulu have you ever made a cake before?" asked Alfie.

"Oh, Alfie! **Anyone** can make a cake," said Lulu.

"Now let's go, go, go!"

Their first stop was
'Sweetness and Bite' where
Miss Rosa sold everything
to do with cakes.

There were so many delicious things to choose from!

"May we have some of those, and some of those, and lots of those, please?"

"Goodness, Lulu!" said Miss Rosa.
"Have you ever made a cake before?"

"Of course!" said Lulu. "Well, not exactly..."

Next they visited Mr Chumpchops the butcher.
"What do you need this for, Lulu?" he asked, handing her a tray.

"We need a **really big** tray for the **really big** cake we're making!" said Lulu. "Do you think we should put sausages in it?"

"Funny sort of cake that would be!" said Mr Chumpchops.

When they got home, Lulu couldn't wait to start. "Come on, Alfie!"

"First, I'm putting all the delicious ingredients in…"

"…and now I'm carefully putting it all in the oven. Oooh la la!

I'm **SO** excited!"

"Then I'm **m_ixing** it all together…"

They got the cake out of the oven just in time.

"It doesn't look **quite** like the picture," said Alfie.

"No one will notice if we cover it with sprinkles!" said Lulu.

"See! It's **perfect!** Let's go, go, **go!**"

Lulu put the cake on Alfie's
scooter.
"We're going to win!
 We're going to win!
   Ours is the **best cake**
     in the **whole world!**"
sang Lulu, all the way
to New Tricks School.

"It's not completely certain,
you know, Lulu," said Alfie.

"Oh, Alfie!" said Lulu.
"Just **wait** till everyone
sees it!"

When they got to school, Dilys, the crossing warden, was helping everyone cross the road safely. All of Lulu's friends were carrying cakes.

Harvey had the tallest cake. "Hallo, Lulu, have you made a cake too?" he asked.

Their teacher, Miss Ellie, welcomed them and told them to take their cakes inside.

"Oh, Miss Ellie!" said Lulu.

"I'm **SO** excited!"

"Oh, yes!"
said Lulu.
"I've made the **best** cake!
Haven't I, Alfie!"

There were some wonderful cakes.

Bonnie had made a cake like a little rocky island in a blue sea.

Pom had made a cake shaped like a bouquet of flowers.

Otto had made a green beetle, just like the ones he collected.

Yumi had made a beautiful Japanese temple cake,

and Harvey had made a soaring skyscraper.

At last, it was Lulu's turn to show **her** cake...

New Tricks Cake Comp

"Ta da!"

she cried
triumphantly.
And there it was.

"Och..."
said Bonnie.

"Oh..."
said Yumi.

"Err..."
said Otto.

"Hmm..."
said Harvey

Miss Ellie stepped forward. "It's time to announce the winner! You have all made wonderful cakes, but the prize for the best cake goes to…"

Lulu closed her eyes tightly and held her breath.

"Umm…" said Pom.

"Oh, dear," said Alfie.

"...**Harvey**," said Miss Ellie, "for his marvellous skyscraper!"

"NOOOOO!"

Lulu let out a wail.
She couldn't help it.

"I'm sorry your cake didn't win," said Harvey.

"It was probably **nearly** the winner," said Yumi.

"I just **really, really** wanted to be the **best!**" sobbed Lulu.

"You don't always have to win, Lulu," said Alfie.

"Winning doesn't matter. We had fun making it, didn't we?"

"Yes, I suppose so," said Lulu sadly.

As they walked back through the park, Alfie said, "You know, Lulu, you're good at **lots** of other things."

"Do you think so?" asked Lulu.

"Definitely," said Alfie. "Especially dancing... oh, look! There's a band playing!"

"Oooh la la!" cried Lulu.

The whole of Wagtail Town had come to see The Beagles.

Everyone was boogying and doogying and

shaking

their

tails!

Lulu
joined
in.

Soon
she
was

twirling...

and

swirling...

and

whirling!

All the
cares of
the day
floated away.

She didn't even notice as everyone
cleared a space all round her to watch.
No one could take their eyes off Lulu.

Bravo, Lulu!

She's amazing!

Wow!

"Lulu is the **best** dancer in Wagtail Town!" said Mr Chumpchops as he handed her a bunch of flowers.

Wonderful!

And **everyone** agreed!

Lulu smiled all the way home.
"Guess what, Alfie!" she said.
"I've had a **really** good idea!"

"Another one?" asked Alfie.

"Yes!" cried Lulu. "Let's all
go to my house and eat
my cake!"

surprisingly good!

And even though Lulu's cake didn't **look** like a winner...
it tasted **delicious!**

So, at the end of another busy day…

The moon came up,
The sun went down,
And all was well
In Wagtail Town.